Racketty-Packetty House

Racketty-Packetty House

As Told by Queen Crosspatch

Frances Hodgson Burnett

Illustrated by

Harrison Cady

DERRYDALE BOOKS
New York • Avenel, New Jersey

This 1992 edition is published by Derrydale Books,

distributed by Outlet Book Company, Inc.,
a Random House Company,
40 Engelhard Avenue, Avenel, New Jersey 07001.

Printed and bound in the United States of America

Book design by Clair Moritz

Library of Congress Cataloging-in-Publication Data

Burnett, Frances Hodgson, 1849-1924.
Racketty-packetty house : as told by Queen Crosspatch /
Frances Hodgson Burnett.
p.   c.m.
Originally published: New York : Century Co., 1906.
Summary: The owner of a tumble-down dollhouse neglects its
shabby occupants for a more aristocratic dollhouse and tenants,
until a princess comes to visit and likes the racketty-packetty
house better.
ISBN 0-517-07249-1
[1. Dolls—Fiction.]   I. Title.
PZ7.B934Rac   1992
[Fic]—dc20   91-30555
CIP
AC

ISBN 0-517-07249-7

8   7   6   5   4   3   2   1

Now this is the story about the doll family I liked and the doll family I didn't. When you read it you are to remember something I am going to tell you. This is it: If you think dolls never do anything you don't see them do, you are very much mistaken. When people are not looking at them they can do anything they choose. They can dance and sing and play on the piano and have all sorts of fun. But they can only move about and talk when people turn their backs and are not looking. If any one looks, they just stop. Fairies know this and of course Fairies visit in all the dolls' houses where the dolls are agreeable. They will not associate, though, with dolls who are not nice. They never call or leave their cards at a dolls' house where the dolls are proud or bad-tempered. They are very particular. If you are conceited or ill-tempered yourself, you will never know a fairy as long as you live.

Queen Crosspatch

RACKETTY-PACKETTY HOUSE was in a corner of Cynthia's nursery. And it was not in the best corner either. It was in the corner behind the door, and that was not at all a fashionable neighborhood. Racketty-Packetty House had been pushed there to be out of the way when Tidy Castle was brought in, on Cynthia's birthday. As soon as she saw Tidy Castle Cynthia did not care for Racketty-Packetty House and indeed was quite ashamed of it. She thought the corner behind the door quite good enough for such a shabby old dolls' house, when there was the beautiful big new one built like a castle and furnished with the most elegant chairs and tables and carpets and curtains and ornaments and pictures and beds and baths and lamps and bookcases, and with a knocker on the front door, and a stable with a pony cart in it at the back. The minute she saw it she called out:

"Oh! what a beautiful doll castle! What shall we do with that untidy old Racketty-Packetty House now? It is too shabby and old-fashioned to stand near it."

In fact, that was the way in which the old dolls' house got its name. It had always been called The Dolls' House, before, but after that it was pushed into the unfashionable neighborhood behind the door and ever afterwards—when it was spoken of at all—it was just called Racketty-Packetty House, and nothing else.

Of course Tidy Castle was grand, and Tidy Castle was new and had all the modern improvements in it, and Racketty-Packetty House was as old-fashioned as it could be. It had belonged to Cynthia's Grandmama and had been made in the days when Queen Victoria was a little girl, and when there were no electric lights even in princesses' dolls' houses. Cynthia's Grandmama had kept it very neat because she had been a good housekeeper even when she was seven years old. But Cynthia was not a good housekeeper and she

Tidy Castle

did not recover the furniture when it got dingy, or repaper the walls, or mend the carpets and bedclothes, and she never thought of such a thing as making new clothes for the doll family, so that of course their early Victorian frocks and capes and bonnets grew in time to be too shabby for words. You see, when Queen Victoria was a little girl, dolls wore queer frocks and long pantalets and boy dolls wore funny frilled trousers and coats which it would almost make you laugh to look at.

But the Racketty-Packetty House family had known better days. I and my Fairies had known them when they were quite new and had been a birthday present just as Tidy Castle was when Cynthia turned eight years old, and there was as much fuss about them when their house arrived as Cynthia made when she saw Tidy Castle.

Cynthia's Grandmama had danced about and clapped her hands with delight, and she had scrambled down upon her knees and taken the dolls out one by one and thought their clothes beautiful. And she had given each one of them a grand name.

"This one shall be Amelia," she said. "And this one is Charlotte, and this is Victoria Leopoldina, and this one Aurelia Matilda, and this one Leontine, and this one Clotilda, and these boys shall be Augustus and Rowland and Vincent and Charles Edward Stuart."

For a long time they led a very gay and fashionable life. They had parties and balls and were presented at Court and went to royal christenings and weddings and were married themselves and had families and scarlet fever and whooping cough and funerals and every luxury. But that was long, long ago, and now all was changed. Their house had grown shabbier and shabbier, and their clothes had grown simply awful. And Aurelia Matilda and Victoria Leopoldina had been broken to bits and thrown into the dustbin, and Leontine—who had really been the beauty of the family—had been dragged out on the hearth rug one night and had had nearly all her paint licked off and a leg chewed up by a Newfoundland puppy, so that she was a sight to behold. As for the boys, Rowland and Vincent had quite disappeared, and Charlotte and Amelia always believed they had run away to seek their fortunes, because things were in such a state at home. So the only ones who were left were Clotilda and Amelia and Charlotte and poor Leontine and Augustus and Charles Edward Stuart. Even they had their names changed.

After Leontine had had her paint licked off so that her head had white bald spots on it and she had scarcely any features, a boy cousin of Cynthia's had put a bright red spot on each cheek and painted her a turned up nose and round saucer blue eyes and a comical mouth. He and Cynthia had called her Ridiklis instead of Leontine, and she had been called that ever since. All the dolls were jointed Dutch dolls, so it was easy to paint any kind of features on them and stick out their arms and legs in any way you liked, and Leontine did look funny after Cynthia's cousin had finished. She certainly was not a beauty but her turned up nose and her round eyes and funny mouth always seemed to be laughing so she really was the most good-natured-looking creature you ever saw.

Charlotte and Amelia, Cynthia had called Meg and Peg, and Clotilda she called Kilmanskeg, and Augustus she called Gustibus, and Charles Edward Stuart was nothing but Peter Piper. So that was the end of their grand names.

The truth was, they went through all sorts of things, and if they had not been such a jolly lot of dolls they might have had fits and appendicitis

Ridiklis

and died of grief. But not a bit of it. If you will believe it, they got fun out of everything. They used to just scream with laughter over the new names, and they laughed so much over them that they got quite fond of them. When Meg's pink silk flounces were torn she pinned them up and didn't mind in the least, and when Peg's lace mantilla was played with by a kitten and brought back to her in rags and tags, she just put a few stitches in it and put it on again; and when Peter Piper lost almost the whole leg of one of his trousers he just laughed and said it made it easier for him to kick about and turn somersaults and he wished the other leg would tear off too.

You never saw a family have such fun. They could make up stories and pretend things and invent games out of nothing. And my Fairies were so fond of them that I couldn't keep them away from the dolls' house. They would go and have fun with Meg and Peg and Kilmanskeg and Gustibus and Peter Piper, even when I had work for them to do in Fairyland. But there, I was so fond of that shabby disrespectable family myself that I never would scold much about them, and I often went to see them. That is how I know so much about them. They were so fond of each other and so good-natured and always in such spirits that everybody who knew them was fond of them. And it was really only Cynthia who didn't know them and thought them only a lot of old disreputable looking Dutch dolls—and Dutch dolls were quite out of fashion. The truth was that Cynthia was not a particularly nice little girl, and did not care much for anything unless it was quite new. But the kitten who had torn the lace mantilla got to know the family and simply loved them all, and the Newfoundland puppy was so sorry about Leontine's paint and her left leg, that he could never do enough to make up. He wanted to marry Leontine as soon as he grew old enough to wear a collar, but Leontine said she would never desert her family, because now that she wasn't the beauty anymore she became the useful one, and did all the kitchen work, and sat up and made poultices and beef tea when any of the rest were ill. And the Newfoundland puppy saw she was right, for the whole family simply adored Ridiklis and could not possibly have done without her. Meg and Peg and Kilmanskeg could have married any minute if they had liked. There were two cock sparrows and a gentleman mouse, who proposed to them over and over again. They all three

Two cock sparrows and a gentleman mouse
proposed to them over and over again

said they did not want fashionable wives but cheerful dispositions and a happy home. But Meg and Peg were like Ridiklis and could not bear to leave their families—besides not wanting to live in nests, and hatch eggs—and Kilmanskeg said she would die of a broken heart if she could not be with Ridiklis, and Ridiklis did not like cheese and crumbs and mousy things, so they could never live together in a mouse hole. But neither the gentleman mouse nor the sparrows were offended because the news was broken to them so sweetly and they went on visiting just as before. Everything was as shabby and disrespectable and as gay and happy as it could be until Tidy Castle was brought into the nursery and then the whole family had rather a fright.

It happened in this way:

When the dolls' house was lifted by the nurse and carried into the corner behind the door, of course it was rather an exciting and shaky thing for Meg and Peg and Kilmanskeg and Gustibus and Peter Piper (Ridiklis was out shopping). The furniture tumbled about and everybody had to hold on to anything they could catch hold of. As it was, Kilmanskeg slid under a table and Peter Piper sat down in the coal-box; but notwithstand-

They did not want fashionable wives, but
cheerful dispositions

ing all this, they did not lose their tempers, and when the nurse sat their house down on the floor with a bump, they all got up and began to laugh. Then they ran and peeped out of the windows and then they ran back and laughed again.

"Well," said Peter Piper, "we have been called Meg and Peg and Kilmanskeg and Gustibus and Peter Piper instead of our grand names, and now we live in a place called Racketty-Packetty House. Who cares! Let's join hands and have a dance."

And they joined hands and danced round and round and kicked up their heels, and their rags and tatters flew about and they laughed until they fell down, one on top of the other.

It was just at this minute that Ridiklis came back. The nurse had found her under a chair and stuck her in through a window. She sat on the drawing room sofa which had holes in its covering and the stuffing coming out, and her one whole leg stuck out straight in front of her, and her bonnet and shawl were on one side and her basket was on her left arm full of things she had got cheap at market. She was out of breath and rather pale through being lifted up and swished through the air so suddenly, but her saucer eyes and her funny mouth looked as cheerful as ever.

"Good gracious, if you knew what I have just heard!" she said. They all scrambled up and called out together.

"Hello! What is it?"

"The nurse said the most awful thing," she answered them. "When Cynthia asked what she should do with this old Racketty-Packetty House, she said, 'Oh! I'll put it behind the door for the present and then it shall be carried downstairs and burned. It's too disgraceful to be kept in any decent nursery.'"

"Oh!" cried out Peter Piper.

"Oh!" said Gustibus.

"Oh! Oh! Oh!" said Meg and Peg and Kilman-skeg. "Will they burn our dear old shabby house? Do you think they will?" And actually tears began to run down their cheeks.

Peter Piper sat down on the floor all at once with his hands stuffed in his pockets.

"I don't care how shabby it is," he said. "It's a jolly nice old place and it's the only house we've ever had."

"I never want to have any other," said Meg.

Gustibus leaned against the wall with his hands stuffed in his pockets.

"I wouldn't move if I was made King of England," he said. "Buckingham Palace wouldn't be half as nice."

"We've had such fun here," said Peg. And Kilmanskeg shook her head from side to side and wiped her eyes on her ragged pocket handkerchief. There is no knowing what would have happened to them if Peter Piper hadn't cheered up as he always did.

"I say," he said, "do you hear that noise?" They all listened and heard a rumbling. Peter Piper ran to the window and looked out and then ran back grinning.

"It's the nurse rolling up the armchair before the house to hide it, so that it won't disgrace the castle. Hooray! Hooray! If they don't see us they will forget all about us and we shall not be burned up at all. Our nice old Racketty-Packetty House will be left alone and we can enjoy ourselves more than ever—because we sha'n't be bothered with Cynthia—Hello! let's all join hands and have a dance."

So they all joined hands and danced round in a ring again and they were so relieved that they laughed and laughed until they all tumbled down in a heap just as they had done before, and rolled

Ridiklis does the cooking

about giggling and squealing. It certainly seemed as if they were quite safe for some time at least. The big easy chair hid them and both the nurse and Cynthia seemed to forget that there was such a thing as a Racketty-Packetty House in the neighborhood. Cynthia was so delighted with Tidy Castle that she played with nothing else for days and days. And instead of being jealous of their grand neighbors the Racketty-Packetty House people began to get all sorts of fun out of watching them from their own windows. Several of their windows were broken and some had rags and paper stuffed into the broken panes, but Meg and Peg and Peter Piper would go and peep out of one, and Gustibus and Kilmanskeg would peep out of another, and Ridiklis could scarcely get her dishes washed and her potatoes pared because she could see the Castle kitchen from her scullery window. It was *so* exciting!

The Castle dolls were grand beyond words, and they were all lords and ladies. These were their names. There was Lady Gwendolen Vere de Vere. She was haughty and had dark eyes and hair and carried her head thrown back and her nose in the air. There was Lady Muriel Vere de Vere, and she was cold and lovely and indifferent and looked down the bridge of her delicate nose. And there was Lady Doris, who had fluffy golden hair and laughed mockingly at everybody. And there was Lord Hubert and Lord Rupert and Lord Francis, who were all handsome enough to make you feel as if you could faint. And there was their mother, the Duchess of Tidyshire; and of course there were all sorts of maids and footmen and cooks and scullery maids and even gardeners.

"We never thought of living to see such grand society," said Peter Piper to his brother and sisters. "It's quite a kind of blessing."

"It's almost like being grand ourselves, just to be able to watch them," said Meg and Peg and Kilmanskeg, squeezing together and flattening their noses against the attic windows.

They could see bits of the sumptuous white and gold drawing room with the Duchess sitting reading near the fire, her golden glasses upon her nose, and Lady Gwendolen playing haughtily upon the harp, and Lady Muriel coldly listening to her. Lady Doris was having her golden hair dressed by her maid in her bedroom and Lord Hubert was reading the newspaper with a high-bred air, while Lord Francis was writing letters to noblemen of his acquaintance, and Lord Rupert was—in an

The Duchess of Tidyshire

aristocratic manner—glancing over his love letters from ladies of title.

Kilmanskeg and Peter Piper just pinched each other with glee and squealed with delight.

"Isn't it fun," said Peter Piper. "I say; aren't they awful swells! But Lord Francis can't kick about in his trousers as I can in mine, and neither can the others. I'll like to see them try to do this"—and he turned three somersaults in the middle of the room and stood on his head on the biggest hole in the carpet—and wiggled his legs and twiggled his toes at them until they shouted so with laughing that Ridiklis ran in with a saucepan in her hand and perspiration on her forehead, because she was cooking turnips, which was all they had for dinner.

"You mustn't laugh so loud," she cried out. "If we make so much noise the Tidy Castle people will begin to complain of this being a low neighborhood and they might insist on moving away."

"Oh! scrump!" said Peter Piper, who sometimes invented doll slang—though there wasn't really a bit of harm in him. "I wouldn't have them move away for anything. They are meat and drink to me."

"They are going to have a dinner of ten

courses," sighed Ridiklis, "I can see them cooking it from my scullery window. And I have nothing but turnips to give you."

"Who cares!" said Peter Piper, "Let's have ten courses of turnips and pretend each course is exactly like the one they are having at the Castle."

"I like turnips almost better than anything—almost—perhaps not quite," said Gustibus. "I can eat ten courses of turnips like a shot."

"Let's go and find out what their courses are," said Meg and Peg and Kilmanskeg, "and then we will write a menu on a piece of pink tissue paper."

And if you'll believe it, that was what they did. They divided their turnips into ten courses and they called the first one Hors d'oeuvres, and the last one Ices, with a French name, and Peter Piper kept jumping up from the table and pretending he was a footman and flourishing about in his flapping rags of trousers and announcing the names of the dishes in such a grand way that they laughed till they nearly died, and said they never had had such a splendid dinner in their lives, and that they would rather live behind the door and watch the Tidy Castle people than be the Tidy Castle people themselves.

And then of course they all joined hands and

Peter Piper announcing the names of the dishes

danced round and round and kicked up their heels for joy, because they always did that whenever there was the least excuse for it—and quite often when there wasn't any at all, just because it was such good exercise and worked off their high spirits so that they could settle down for a while.

This was the way things went on day after day. They almost lived at their windows. They watched the Tidy Castle family get up and be dressed by their maids and valets in different clothes almost every day. They saw them drive out in their carriages, and have parties, and go to balls. They all nearly had brain fever with delight the day they watched Lady Gwendolen and Lady Muriel and Lady Doris, dressed in their Court trains and feathers, going to be presented at the first drawing room.

After the lovely creatures had gone the whole family sat down in a circle round the Racketty-Packetty House library fire, and Ridiklis read aloud to them about drawing rooms, out of a scrap of the *Lady's Pictorial* she had found, and after that they had a Court drawing room of their own, and they made tissue paper trains and glass bead crowns for diamond tiaras, and sometimes Gustibus pretended to be the royal family, and the others were presented to him and kissed his hand, and then the others took turns and he was presented. And suddenly the most delightful thing occurred to Peter Piper. He thought it would be rather nice to make them all into lords and ladies and he did it by touching them on the shoulder with the drawing room poker which he straightened because it was so crooked that it was almost bent double. It was not exactly the way such things are done at Court, but Peter Piper thought it would do—and at any rate it was great fun. So he made them all kneel down in a row and he touched each on the shoulder with the poker and said:

"Rise up, Lady Meg and Lady Peg and Lady Kilmanskeg and Lady Ridiklis of Racketty-Packetty House—and also the Right Honorable Lord Gustibus Rags!" And they all jumped up at once and made bows and curtsied to each other. But they made Peter Piper into a Duke, and he was called the Duke of Tags. He knelt down on the big hole in the carpet and each one of them gave him a little thump on the shoulder with the poker, because it took more thumps to make a Duke than a common or garden Lord.

The day after this another much more exciting

The Duke of Tags

thing took place. The nurse was in a bad temper and when she was tidying the nursery she pushed the easy chair aside and saw Racketty-Packetty House.

"Oh!" she said, "there is that Racketty-Packetty old thing still. I had forgotten it. It must be carried downstairs and burned. I will go and tell one of the footmen to come for it."

Meg and Peg and Kilmanskeg were in their attic and they all rushed out in such a hurry to get downstairs that they rolled all the way down the staircase, and Peter Piper and Gustibus had to dart out of the drawing room and pick them up, Ridiklis came staggering up from the kitchen quite out of breath.

"Oh! our house is going to be burned! Our house is going to be burned!" cried Meg and Peg clutching their brothers.

"Let us go and throw ourselves out of the window!" cried Kilmanskeg.

"I don't see how they can have the heart to burn a person's home!" said Ridiklis, wiping her eyes with her kitchen duster.

Peter Piper was rather pale, but he was extremely brave and remembered that he was the head of the family.

"Now, Lady Meg and Lady Peg and Lady Kilmanskeg," he said, "let us all keep cool."

"We shan't keep cool when they set our house on fire," said Gustibus. Peter Piper just snapped his fingers.

"Pooh!" he said. "We are only made of wood and it won't hurt a bit. We shall just snap and crackle and go off almost like fireworks and then we shall be ashes and fly away into the air and see all sorts of things. Perhaps it may be more fun than anything we have done yet."

"But our nice old house! Our nice old Racketty-Packetty House," said Ridiklis. "I do so love it. The kitchen is so convenient—even though the oven won't bake anymore."

And things looked most serious because the nurse really was beginning to push the armchair away. But it would not move and I will tell you why. One of my Fairies, who had come down the chimney when they were talking, had called me and I had come in a second with a whole army of my Workers, and though the nurse couldn't see them, they were all holding the chair tight down on the carpet so that it would not stir.

And I—Queen Crosspatch—myself—flew downstairs and made the footman remember that

Queen Crosspatch makes the footman remember
Cynthia's box

minute that a box had come for Cynthia and that he must take it upstairs to her nursery. If I had not been on the spot he would have forgotten it until it was too late. But just in the very nick of time up he came, and Cynthia sprang up as soon as she saw him.

"Oh!" she cried out, "It must be the doll who broke her little leg and was sent to the hospital. It must be Lady Patsy."

And she opened the box and gave a little scream of joy for there lay Lady Patsy (her whole name was Patricia) in a lace-frilled nightgown, with her lovely leg in bandages and a pair of tiny crutches and a trained nurse by her side.

That was how I saved them that time. There was such excitement over Lady Patsy and her little crutches and her nurse that nothing else was thought of and my Fairies pushed the armchair back and Racketty-Packetty House was hidden and forgotten once more.

The whole Racketty-Packetty family gave a great gasp of joy and sat down in a ring all at once, on the floor, mopping their foreheads with anything they could get hold of. Peter Piper used an antimacassar.

"Oh! we are obliged to you, Queen B-bell—

Patch," he panted out, "But these alarms of fire are upsetting."

"You leave them to me," I said, "and I'll attend to them. Tip!" I commanded the Fairy nearest me. "You will have to stay about here and be ready to give the alarm when anything threatens to happen." And I flew away, feeling I had done a good morning's work. Well, that was the beginning of a great many things, and many of them were connected with Lady Patsy; and but for me there might have been unpleasantness.

Of course the Racketty-Packetty dolls forgot about their fright directly, and began to enjoy themselves again as usual. That was their way. They never sat up all night with Trouble, Peter Piper used to say. And I told him they were quite right. If you make a fuss over trouble and put it to bed and nurse it and give it beef tea and gruel, you can never get rid of it.

Their great delight now was Lady Patsy. They thought she was prettier than any of the other Tidy Castle dolls. She neither turned her nose up, nor looked down the bridge of it, nor laughed mockingly. She had dimples in the corners of her mouth and long curly lashes and her nose was saucy and her eyes were bright and full of laughs.

"She's the clever one of the family," said Peter Piper. "I am sure of that."

She was treated as an invalid at first, of course, and kept in her room; but they could see her sitting up in her frilled nightgown. After a few days she was carried to a soft chair by the window and there she used to sit and look out; and the Racketty-Packetty House dolls crowded round their window and adored her.

After a few days, they noticed that Peter Piper was often missing and one morning Ridiklis went up into the attic and found him sitting at a window all by himself and staring and staring.

"Oh! Duke," she said (you see they always tried to remember each other's titles). "Dear me, Duke, what are you doing here?"

"I am looking at her," he answered. "I'm in love. I fell in love with her the minute Cynthia took her out of her box. I am going to marry her."

"But she's a lady of high degree," said Ridiklis quite alarmed.

"That's why she'll have me," said Peter Piper in his most cheerful manner. "Ladies of high degree always marry the good-looking ones in rags and tatters. If I had a whole suit of clothes on, she wouldn't look at me. I'm very good-looking, you

Racketty-Packetty House

know," and he turned round and winked at Ridiklis in such a delightful saucy way that she suddenly felt as if he *was* very good-looking, though she had not thought of it before.

"Hello," he said all at once. "I've just thought of something to attract her attention. Where's the ball of string?"

Cynthia's kitten had made them a present of a ball of string which had been most useful. Ridiklis ran and got it, and all the others came running upstairs to see what Peter Piper was going to do. They all were delighted to hear he had fallen in love with the lovely, funny Lady Patsy. They found him standing in the middle of the attic unrolling the ball of string.

"What are you going to do, Duke?" they all shouted.

"Just you watch," he said, and he began to make the string into a rope ladder—as fast as lightning. When he had finished it, he fastened one end of it to a beam and swung the other end out of the window.

"From her window," he said, "she can see Racketty-Packetty House and I'll tell you something. She's always looking at it. She watches us as much as we watch her, and I have seen her giggling and giggling when we were having fun. Yesterday when I chased Lady Meg and Lady Peg and Lady Kilmanskeg round and round the front of the house and turned somersaults every five steps, she laughed until she had to stuff her handkerchief into her mouth. When we joined hands and danced and laughed until we fell in heaps I thought she was going to have a kind of rosy-dimpled, lovely little fit, she giggled so. If I run down the side of the house on this rope ladder it will attract her attention and then I shall begin to do things."

He ran down the ladder and that very minute they saw Lady Patsy at her window give a start and lean forward to look. They all crowded round their window and chuckled and chuckled as they watched him.

He turned three stately somersaults and stood on his feet and made a cheerful bow. The Racketty-Packettys saw Lady Patsy begin to giggle that minute. Then he took an antimacassar out of his pocket and fastened it round the edge of his torn trousers leg, as if it were lace trimming and began to walk about like a Duke—with his arms folded on his chest and his ragged old hat cocked on one side over his ear. Then the Racketty-Packettys

They all crowded round their window and
chuckled and chuckled as they watched him

saw Lady Patsy begin to laugh. Then Peter Piper stood on his head and kissed his hand and Lady Patsy covered her face and rocked backwards and forwards in her chair laughing and laughing.

Then he struck an attitude with his tattered leg put forward gracefully and he pretended he had a guitar and he sang—right up at her window.

> From Racketty-Packetty House I come,
> It stands, dear Lady, in a slum,
> A low, low slum behind the door
> The stout armchair is placed before,
> (Just take a look at it, my Lady).
> The house itself is a perfect sight,
> And everybody's dressed like a perfect fright,
> But no one cares a single jot
> And each one giggles over his lot,
> (And as for me, I'm in love with you).
> I can't make up another verse,
> And if I did it would be worse,
> But I could stand and sing all day,
> If I could think of things to say,
> (But the fact is I just wanted to
> make you look at me).

And then he danced such a lively jig that his rags and tags flew about him, and then he made another bow and kissed his hand again and ran up the ladder like a flash and jumped into the attic.

After that Lady Patsy sat at her window all the time and would not let the trained nurse put her to bed at all; and Lady Gwendolen and Lady Muriel and Lady Doris could not understand it. Once Lady Gwendolen said haughtily and disdainfully and scornfully and scathingly:

"If you sit there so much, those low Racketty-Packetty House people will think you are looking at them."

"I am," said Lady Patsy, showing all her dimples at once. "They are such fun."

And Lady Gwendolen swooned haughtily away, and the trained nurse could scarcely restore her.

When the Castle dolls drove out or walked in their garden, the instant they caught sight of one of the Racketty-Packettys they turned up their noses and sniffed aloud, and several times the Duchess said she would remove because the neighborhood was absolutely low. They all scorned the Racketty-Packettys—they just *scorned* them.

One moonlight night Lady Patsy was sitting at her window and she heard a whistle in the garden. When she peeped out carefully, there stood

39

Peter Piper waving his ragged cap at her, and he had his rope ladder under his arm.

"Hello," he whispered as loud as he could. "Could you catch a bit of rope if I threw it up to you?"

"Yes," she whispered back.

"Then catch this," he whispered again and he threw up the end of a string and she caught it the first throw. It was fastened to the rope ladder.

"Now pull," he said.

She pulled and pulled until the rope ladder reached her window and then she fastened that to a hook under the sill and the first thing that happened—just like lightning—was that Peter Piper ran up the ladder and leaned over her window ledge.

"Will you marry me?" he said. "I haven't anything to give you to eat and I am as ragged as a scarecrow, but-will you?"

She clapped her little hands.

"I eat very little," she said. "And I would do without anything at all, if I could live in your funny old shabby house."

"It is a ridiculous, tumbled-down old barn, isn't it?" he said. "But every one of us is as nice as we can be. We are perfect Turkish Delights. It's

"Will you marry me?" he said

laughing that does it. Would you like to come down the ladder and see what a jolly, shabby old hole the place is?"

"Oh! do take me," said Lady Patsy.

So he helped her down the ladder and took her under the armchair and into Racketty-Packetty House and Meg and Peg and Kilmanskeg and Ridiklis and Gustibus all crowded round her and gave little screams of joy at the sight of her.

They were afraid to kiss her at first, even though she was engaged to Peter Piper. She was so pretty and her frock had so much lace on it that they were afraid their old rags might spoil her. But she did not care about her lace and flew at them and kissed and hugged them every one.

"I have so wanted to come here," she said. "It's so dull at the Castle I had to break my leg just to get a change. The Duchess sits reading near the fire with her gold eyeglasses on her nose and Lady Gwendolen plays haughtily on the harp and Lady Muriel coldly listens to her, and Lady Doris is always laughing mockingly, and Lord Hubert reads the newspaper with a high-bred air, and Lord Francis writes letters to noblemen of his ac-quaintance, and Lord Rupert glances over his love letters from ladies of title, in an aristocratic man-

Lord Rupert glances over his love letters

ner—until I could *scream*. Just to see you dears dancing about in your rags and tags and laughing and inventing games as if you didn't mind anything, is such a relief."

She nearly laughed her little curly head off when they all went round the house with her, and Peter Piper showed her the holes in the carpet and the stuffing coming out of the sofas, and the feathers out of the beds, and the legs tumbling off the chairs. She had never seen anything like it before.

"At the Castle, nothing is funny at all," she said. "And nothing ever sticks out or hangs down or tumbles off. It is so plain and new."

"But I think we ought to tell her, Duke," Ridiklis said. "We may have our house burned over our heads any day." She really stopped laughing for a whole minute when she heard that, but she was rather like Peter Piper in disposition and she said almost immediately.

"Oh! they'll never do it. They've forgotten you." And Peter Piper said:

"Don't let's think of it. Let's all join hands and dance round and round and kick up our heels and laugh as hard as ever we can."

And they did—and Lady Patsy laughed harder

than any one else. After that she was always stealing away from Tidy Castle and coming in and having fun. Sometimes she stayed all night and slept with Meg and Peg and everybody invented new games and stories and they really never went to bed until daylight. But the Castle dolls grew more and more scornful every day, and tossed their heads higher and higher and sniffed louder and louder until it sounded as if they all had influenza. They never lost an opportunity of saying disdainful things and once the Duchess wrote a letter to Cynthia, saying that she insisted on removing to a decent neighborhood. She laid the letter in her desk but the gentleman mouse came in the night and carried it away. So Cynthia never saw it and I don't believe she could have read it if she had seen it because the Duchess wrote very badly—even for a doll.

And then what do you suppose happened? One morning Cynthia began to play that all the Tidy Castle dolls had scarlet fever. She said it had broken out in the night and she undressed them all and put them into bed and gave them medicine. She could not find Lady Patsy, so *she* escaped the contagion. The truth was that Lady Patsy had stayed all night at Racketty-Packetty House,

The gentleman mouse brought the shavings
from his nest

where they were giving an imitation Court Ball with Peter Piper in a tin crown, and shavings for supper—because they had nothing else, and in fact the gentleman mouse had brought the shavings from his nest as a present.

Cynthia played nearly all day and the Duchess and Lady Gwendolen and Lady Muriel and Lady Doris and Lord Hubert and Lord Francis and Lord Rupert got worse and worse.

By evening they were all raging in delirium and Lord Francis and Lady Gwendolen had strong mustard plasters on their chests. And right in the middle of their agony Cynthia suddenly got up and went away and left them to their fate—just as if it didn't matter in the least. Well in the middle of the night Meg and Peg and Lady Patsy wakened all at once.

"Do you hear a noise?" said Meg, lifting her head from her ragged old pillow.

"Yes, I do," said Peg, sitting up and holding her ragged old blanket up to her chin.

Lady Patsy jumped up with feathers sticking up all over her hair, because they had come out of the holes in the ragged old bed. She ran to the window and listened.

"Oh! Meg and Peg!" she cried out. "It comes

from the Castle. Cynthia has left them all raving in delirium and they are all shouting and groaning and screaming."

Meg and Peg jumped up too.

"Let's go and call Kilmanskeg and Ridiklis and Gustibus and Peter Piper," they said, and they rushed to the staircase and met Kilmanskeg and Ridiklis and Gustibus and Peter Piper coming scrambling up panting because the noise had wakened them as well.

They were all over at Tidy Castle in a minute. They just tumbled over each other to get there—the kind-hearted things. The servants were every one fast asleep, though the noise was awful. The loudest groans came from Lady Gwendolen and Lord Francis because their mustard plasters were blistering them frightfully.

Ridiklis took charge, because she was the one who knew most about illness. She sent Gustibus to waken the servants and then ordered hot water and cold water, and ice, and brandy, and poultices, and shook the trained nurse for not attending to her business—and took off the mustard plasters and gave gruel and broth and cough syrup and castor oil and ipecacuanha, and every one of the Racketty-Packettys massaged, and soothed,

"Do you hear a noise?" said Meg

and patted, and put wet cloths on heads, until the fever was gone and the Castle dolls all lay back on their pillows pale and weak, but smiling faintly at every Racketty-Packetty they saw, instead of turning up their noses and tossing their heads and sniffing loudly, and just *scorning* them.

Lady Gwendolen spoke first and instead of being haughty and disdainful, she was as humble as a newborn kitten.

"Oh you dear, shabby, disrespectful, darling things!" she said. "Never, never, will I scorn you again. Never, never!"

"That's right!" said Peter Piper in his cheerful, rather slangy way. "You take my tip—never you scorn anyone again. It's a mistake. Just you watch me stand on my head. It'll cheer you up."

And he turned six somersaults—just like lightning—and stood on his head and wiggled his ragged legs at them until suddenly they heard a snort from one of the beds and it was Lord Hubert beginning to laugh and then Lord Francis laughed and then Lord Hubert shouted, and then Lady Doris squealed, and Lady Muriel screamed, and Lady Gwendolen and the Duchess rolled over and over in their beds, laughing as if they would have fits.

"Oh! you delightful, funny, shabby old loves!" Lady Gwendolen kept saying. "To think that we scorned you."

"They'll be all right after this," said Peter Piper. "There's nothing cures scarlet fever like cheering up. Let's all join hands and dance round and round once for them before we go back to bed. It'll throw them into a nice light perspiration and they'll drop off and sleep like tops." And they did it, and before they had finished, the whole lot of them were perspiring gently and snoring as softly as lambs.

When they went back to Racketty-Packetty House they talked a good deal about Cynthia and wondered and wondered why she had left her scarlet fever so suddenly. And at last Ridiklis made up her mind to tell them something she had heard.

"The Duchess told me," she said, rather slowly because it was bad news—"The Duchess said that Cynthia went away because her mama had sent for her—and her mama had sent for her to tell her that a little girl princess is coming to see her tomorrow. Cynthia's Mama used to be a maid of honor to the Queen and that's why the little girl princess is coming. The Duchess said—" and here

Ridiklis spoke very slowly indeed, "that the nurse was so excited she said she did not know whether she stood on her head or her heels, and she must tidy up the nursery and have that Racketty-Packetty old dolls' house carried down stairs and burned, early tomorrow morning. That's what the Duchess *said*—"

Meg and Peg and Kilmanskeg clutched at their hearts and gasped and Gustibus groaned and Lady Patsy caught Peter Piper by the arm to keep from falling. Peter Piper gulped—and then he had a sudden cheerful thought.

"Perhaps she was raving in delirium," he said.

"No, she wasn't," said Ridiklis shaking her head, "I had just given her hot water and cold, and gruel, and broth, and castor oil, and ipecacuanha and put ice almost all over her. She was as sensible as any of us. Tomorrow morning we shall not have a house over our heads," and she put her ragged old apron over her face and cried.

"If she wasn't raving in delirium," said Peter Piper, "we shall not have any heads. You had better go back to the Castle tonight, Patsy. Racketty-Packetty House is no place for you."

Then Lady Patsy drew herself up so straight that she nearly fell over backwards.

"Oh you dear, shabby, disrespectable,
darling things!" she said

"I—will—*never*—leave you;" she said, and Peter Piper couldn't make her.

You can just imagine what a doleful night it was. They went all over the house together and looked at every hole in the carpet and every piece of stuffing sticking out of the dear old shabby sofas, and every broken window and chair leg and table and ragged blanket—and the tears ran down their faces for the first time in their lives. About six o'clock in the morning Peter Piper made a last effort.

"Let's all join hands in a circle," he said quite faintly, "and dance round and round once more."

But it was no use. When they joined hands they could not dance, and when they found they could not dance they all tumbled down in a heap and cried instead of laughing, and Lady Patsy lay with her arms round Peter Piper's neck.

Now here is where I come in again—Queen Crosspatch—who is telling you this story. I always come in just at the nick of time when people like the Racketty-Packettys are in trouble. I walked in at seven o'clock.

"Get up off the floor," I said to them all and they got up and stared at me. They actually thought I did not know what had happened.

She put her ragged old apron over her face
and cried

"A little girl princess is coming this morning," said Peter Piper, "and our house is going to be burned over our heads. This is the end of Rack-etty-Packetty House."

"No, it isn't!" I said. "You leave this to me. I told the princess to come here, though she doesn't know it in the least."

A whole army of my Working Fairies began to swarm in at the nursery window. The nurse was working very hard to put things in order. She had not sense enough to see Fairies at all so she did not see mine, though there were hundreds of them. As soon as she made one corner tidy, they ran after her and made it untidy. They held her back by her dress and hung and swung on her apron until she could scarcely move and kept wondering why she was so slow. She could not make the nursery tidy and she was so flurried she forgot all about Racketty-Packetty House again— especially as my Working Fairies pushed the arm-chair close up to it so that it was quite hidden. And there it was when the little girl princess came with her ladies in waiting. My fairies had only just allowed the nurse to finish the nursery.

Meg and Peg and Kilmanskeg and Ridiklis and Gustibus and Peter Piper and Lady Patsy were huddled up together looking out of one window. They could not bear to be parted. I sat on the arm of the big chair and ordered my Working Fairies to stand ready to obey me the instant I spoke.

The princess was a nice child and was very polite to Cynthia when she showed her all her dolls, and last but not least, Tidy Castle itself. She looked at all the rooms and the furniture and said polite and admiring things about each of them. But Cynthia realized that she was not so much interested in it as she had thought she would be. The fact was that the princess had so many grand dolls' houses in her palace that Tidy Castle did not surprise her at all. It was just when Cynthia was finding this out that I gave the order to my Working Fairies.

"Push the armchair away," I commanded; "very slowly, so that no one will know it is being moved."

So they moved it away—very, very slowly—and no one saw that it had stirred. But the next minute the little girl princess gave a delightful start.

"Oh! What is that!" she cried out, hurrying towards the unfashionable neighborhood behind the door.

They went all over the house together

Cynthia blushed all over and the nurse actually turned pale. The Racketty-Packettys tumbled down in a heap beneath their window and began to say their prayers very fast.

"It is only a shabby old doll's house, your Highness," Cynthia stammered out. "It belonged to my grandmama, and it ought not to be in the nursery. I thought you had had it burned, Nurse!"

"Burned!" the little girl princess cried out in the most shocked way. "Why if it was mine, I wouldn't have it burned for worlds! Oh! please push the chair away and let me look at it. There are no doll's houses like it anywhere in these days." And when the armchair was pushed aside she scrambled down onto her knees just as if she were not a little girl princess at all.

"Oh! Oh! Oh!" she said. "How funny and dear! What a darling old doll's house. It is shabby and wants mending, of course, but it is almost exactly like one my grandmama had—she kept it among her treasures and only let me look at it as a great, great treat."

Cynthia gave a gasp, for the little girl princess's grandmama had been the queen and people had knelt down and kissed her hand and had been obliged to go out of the room backwards before her.

The little girl princess was simply filled with joy. She picked up Meg and Peg and Kilmanskeg and Gustibus and Peter Piper as if they had been really a queen's dolls.

"Oh! the darling dears," she said. "Look at their nice, queer faces and their funny clothes. Just—just like Grandmama's dollies' clothes. Only these poor things do so want new ones. Oh! how I should like to dress them again just as they used to be dressed, and have the house all made just as it used to be when it was new."

"That old Racketty-Packetty House," said Cynthia, losing her breath.

"If it were mine I should make it just like Grandmama's and I should love it more than any doll's house I have. I never—never—never—saw anything as nice and laughing and good-natured as these dolls' faces. They look as if they had been having fun ever since they were born. Oh! if you were to burn them and their home I—I could never forgive you!"

"I never—never—will—your Highness," stammered Cynthia, quite overwhelmed. Suddenly she started forward.

"Why, there is the lost doll!" she cried out.

"Oh! the darling dears," she said

"There is Lady Patsy. How did she get into Rack-etty-Packetty House?"

"Perhaps she went there to see them because they were so poor and shabby," said the little girl Princess. "Perhaps she likes this one," and she pointed to Peter Piper. "Do you know when I picked him up their arms were about each other. Please let her stay with him. Oh!" she cried out the next instant and jumped a little. "I felt as if the boy one kicked his leg."

And it was actually true, because Peter Piper could not help it and he had kicked out his ragged leg for joy. He had to be very careful not to kick any more when he heard what happened next.

As the Princess liked Racketty-Packetty House so much, Cynthia gave it to her for a present—and the princess was really happy—and before she went away she made a little speech to the whole Racketty-Packetty family, whom she had set all in a row in the ragged old, dear old, shabby old drawing room where they had had so much fun.

"You are going to come and live with me, funny, good-natured loves," she said. "And you shall all be dressed beautifully again and your house shall be mended and papered and painted and made as lovely as ever it was. And I am going

They used to make deep curtseys when a Racketty
Packetty doll passed

to like you better than all my other dolls' houses —just as Grandmama said she liked hers." And then she was gone.

And every bit of it came true. Racketty-Packetty House was carried to a splendid nursery in a palace, and Meg and Peg and Kilmanskeg and Ridiklis and Gustibus and Peter Piper were made so gorgeous that if they had not been so nice they would have grown proud. But they didn't. They only grew jollier and jollier and Peter Piper married Lady Patsy, and Ridiklis's left leg was mended and she was painted into a beauty again—but she always remained the useful one. And the dolls in the other dolls' houses used to make deep curtseys when a Racketty-Packetty House doll passed them, and Peter Piper could scarcely stand it because it always made him want to stand on his head and laugh—and so when they were curtsied at—because they were related to the royal dolls' house—they used to run into their drawing room and fall into fits of giggles and they could only stop them by all joining hands together in a ring and dancing round and round and round and kicking up their heels and laughing until they tumbled down in a heap.

And what do you think of that for a story?

Doesn't it prove to you what a valuable friend a Fairy is—particularly a queen one?